Santa's Christmas Genies

Adapted by Hollis James
from the script "My Secret Genies" by Sindy Boveda Spackman

Illustrated by Mattia Francesco Laviosa

A GOLDEN BOOK • NEW YORK

randomhousekids.com
ISBN 978-0-399-55121-5
Printed in the United States of America
10 9 8 7 6 5 4 3 2 1

It was the day before Christmas, and Leah had almost finished writing her letter to Santa when her neighbor Zac knocked at the door. He needed stamps for his own letter to Santa.

"All I want for Christmas is a canoe," he said.

"I'm asking Santa for snow on Christmas," Leah said, holding up her snowflake-shaped letter.

Zac wanted to get home to make room for his canoe, so Leah offered to mail his letter to Santa for him.

The mail truck arrived, and Leah ran to meet it. But when she returned to her house, she saw Zac's letter on the ground. She'd dropped it! Now her friend wouldn't get his Christmas canoe.

"If only I had a way to get this to Santa before Christmas," she said. Then she realized she did—her magical genies-in-training, Shimmer and Shine!

She called for them, and they appeared in a *poof* of sparkles with their pets, Tala and Nahal.

Shimmer and Shine didn't know what Christmas was, so Leah explained it to them.

"First you write a letter to Santa about what you want for Christmas. Then Santa's elves make the presents in his workshop for Santa to deliver by Christmas morning!"

The genies were happy to help Leah.

"Boom, Zahramay!" Shimmer chanted. *"First wish of the day! Shimmer and Shine, get this letter to Santa divine!"*

Suddenly, Leah and the genies, along with Tala and Nahal, were standing in the snowy North Pole.

"I just wanted to get the letter to Santa," Leah said. "I didn't think I'd be giving it to him in person!"

"Oh, snowball!" said Shimmer. "My mistake, Leah."

"This mistake is great!" exclaimed Leah. "Because now I get to meet Santa!"

Leah and her friends found Santa's workshop. The elves invited them in and gave them hot chocolate so they could warm up.

"I love hot chocolate!" said Shimmer. "There are even tiny marshmallows in it . . . shaped like tiny mugs of hot chocolate!"

"This Santa fella really knows how to live," said Shine.

"Why, thank you, Shine!" said a booming, jolly voice. It was Santa!

"How do you know my name?"
asked Shine.

"I know every child in the world,
even the genies in Zahramay
Falls," replied Santa. "But you
need a genie bottle to get to
Zahramay Falls, and I don't have
one. If I did, I'd bring you presents
every day to make up for all the
genie Christmases I've missed!"

Leah gave Zac's letter to Santa. But Santa already knew about the canoe. "Zac's been sending me a letter every day since last Christmas!" he said, chuckling.

Santa gave Leah and the genies a tour of his workshop. They saw busy elves making toys, and the reindeer who pulled his sleigh.

At the end of the tour, Santa said, "I hope you enjoyed visiting my workshop."

"We did," said Leah, shivering. "I wish you lived someplace warmer, though."

"Boom, Zahramay! Second wish of the day!" Shine chanted. *"Shimmer and Shine, get Santa someplace warmer divine!"*

Whoosh! Santa was whisked away to a tropical island.

"I didn't mean to make *that* wish!" cried Leah.
"Not when Santa still has presents to deliver."

"Oh, right," said Shine. "I forgot about that part. My mistake."

When the elves heard that Santa was gone, they started to panic.

"I wish these elves would calm down!" said Leah.

"Boom, Zahramay, third wish of the day!" Shimmer sang. "Shimmer and Shine, elves calm down divine!"

With those words, the elves fell into a deep sleep.

"That was my last wish!" exclaimed Leah. "We need those elves to be awake so they can finish the presents."

"Oh, sleigh bells," cried Shimmer. "My mistake, Leah. I thought that's what you wished for."

"I did," replied Leah. "So it was *my* mistake. Maybe it'll be all right—as long as we finish these presents and find Santa!"

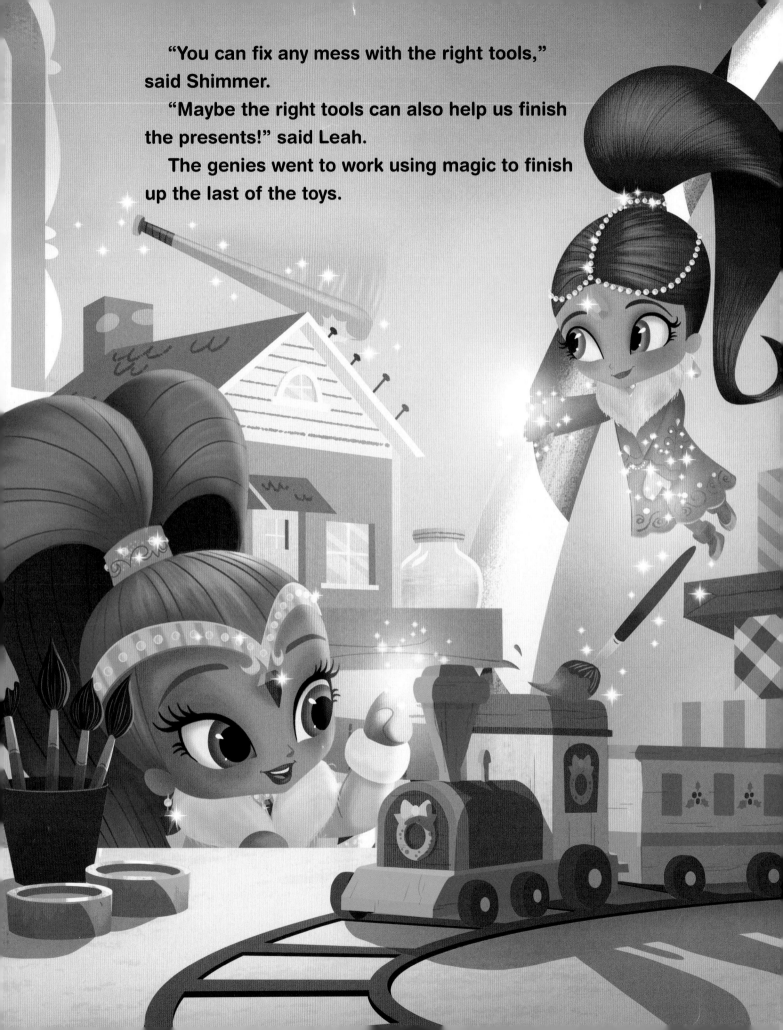

"You can fix any mess with the right tools," said Shimmer.

"Maybe the right tools can also help us finish the presents!" said Leah.

The genies went to work using magic to finish up the last of the toys.

The gifts were loaded onto Santa's sleigh. It was time to make the deliveries, but the genies weren't sure where to go.

"Maybe we should press this button with the picture of Santa on it!" said Shine.

"Don't press the button," warned Leah and Shimmer.

But Shine couldn't help herself. "I'm pressing the button!"

Shine had pressed the Santa-tracking button. The reindeer
leapt into the air and flew Leah and her friends right to the
beach where Santa was stranded.

The sleigh crashed to a stop in the sand. Leah and her friends tried to get the sleigh out, but it was stuck.

"If only we had something else that Santa could fly," said Leah.

"How about a magic carpet?" suggested Shimmer.

Together the sisters chanted: *"Shimmer and Shine, double genie magic divine!"*

Poof! Santa was back in his red suit and perched on a magic carpet.

"Ho, ho, ho!" he exclaimed. "It's time to save Christmas!"

Flying from house to house, Leah, Shimmer, and Shine helped Santa deliver presents all around the world.

When all the gifts had been delivered, Santa took Leah home.

"Santa, thank you so much for everything," said Leah.

"You're welcome," he replied. "But I still have one more present in my bag."

He pulled Leah's snowflake-shaped letter out of his bag
and sent it into the sky. It vanished in a burst of sparkles,
and snow started to fall. Soon the entire street was covered
in a beautiful blanket of white!

"It's snowing for Christmas morning!" said Leah. It was
just what she wanted!

"We fixed our mistakes, and the day turned out great!" Leah exclaimed as Santa and the genies flew away. At that very moment, Zac ran up carrying something really big.

"I got my canoe!" he announced. "And you got what you wanted, too, Leah! Santa totally crushed it this year!"

Meanwhile, the genies and Santa returned to the tropical island and freed his sleigh. To thank them, Santa gave them a gift—a hot-chocolate maker! And they had a gift for him, too—a genie bottle!

"Now you can bring Christmas to Zahramay Falls!" Shine said.

"Of all the presents in the world, this one is my favorite," declared Santa. "Merry Christmas, Shimmer and Shine!"

Shimmer and Shine flew away on their magic carpet. As they sailed out of sight, they sang:
"We saved the day with three merry wishes!
Boom, Zahramay! We'll see you next Christmas!"